David's Bride

Book Three in the Millshore Brides

Kirsten Osbourne

Chapter One

Grace and her best friend Sadie sagged for a moment over their looms in the Millshore Textile Mill. It was their last day of work for the week, and they were both happy to hear the bell that signified the end of their workday.

Grace stood up after a moment and held out her hand to pull Sadie to her feet. Poor Sadie hadn't been feeling well all week, and it was difficult for her to keep working. "I can't believe you worked every day this week. Are you feeling any better?"

Sadie looked at her friend's face and nodded. "I think so. Maybe. I need some sunshine. Maybe we should take the long way home and just bask in the sun."

Grace wanted to wrinkle her nose. It was too cold outside to be basking in the sun. As they stepped outside, there was no sun in sight. It was a dreary winter day. "I think I'm going to put an ad in the paper for a husband, like Josephine and Rebecca. In their letters to us, they both seem so happy. Mrs. Durant is a godsend, helping us all find husbands, so we don't have to work so hard in the mill."

Sadie frowned. "I hate the idea of you going away!"

Grace nodded. She knew she'd feel the same if it was Sadie leaving. "I know. I hate to leave you, but...I'm not going to work in that mill one day more than I need to." Her parents had died when she was a little girl, and she and Sadie had met in the orphanage she'd been placed in. Since neither of them was married when they aged out of the orphanage at fourteen, the matron there had found them their positions at the mill.

"How am I supposed to live without you by my side?" Sadie asked, her voice weaker than it should have been due to the cold she'd had.

"I'll write you at least once a week...pages and pages! It'll be like I never left."

Sadie frowned for a moment. "Perhaps you can find a man for me when you arrive? That would be wonderful."

"I'll do my very best!" Grace didn't tell her friend that she'd already put an ad in the papers. She didn't want Sadie to feel as if she'd hidden something from her.

"Then we can be together again."

"I want nothing more." Except to get out of the mill. That she wanted more than anything on earth.

They walked along the river and finally went into the boarding house where they shared a room with two other girls. There had been six of them just a short while before, but two had gone off to be mail order brides. Now Grace was going to follow in their footsteps.

Everyone was already at the table for supper when the two girls rushed in. "I didn't realize we were so late!" Grace said. "It's my fault." She hurried upstairs to wash her hands and face for supper, aware that Sadie was right behind her.

After they'd both cleaned up, they hurried down and took their places at the table. Grace could see the corner of an envelope sticking out from under her plate.

Mrs. Durant had made chicken and dumplings for supper. Very little chicken and a lot of dumplings, so the meal was affordable, and they wouldn't go hungry. Grace sniffed the air and sighed happily. This was one of her favorite meals.

Mrs. Durant said grace for them, and cheerful voices filled the room. They all worked in the mill all day, but they refused to let the mill bring them down. Instead, they worked at keeping their moods happy. What else could they do? There was no point in letting the mill control everything about them when they had the ability to keep one another cheerful.

Grace eyed the letter once more, and finally, she couldn't bear it. She pulled it out and read its contents while eating. The words drowned out the chatter around her.

Dear Miss Grace Hart,

I saw your advertisement in the newspaper, and I just had to respond. I live in a relatively new community that was built right along the Oregon Trail. I've always known I would meet my wife in one of the groups traveling along the trail, but the Oregon Trail seems to have been forgotten now that the railroads have taken over.

I have a small spread of land that borders on my sister and brother-in-law's land. You will find that it's easy to make friends here. I live alone, but still take most of my meals at my sister's house. I'm not a good cook, but that's where I hope you'll come in.

My name is David Jack Smith. I'm a farmer. I'm twenty-four years old. I have all my teeth and my hair is brown. I love our little community here in Clover Creek, but I feel as if I need to look outside our people for a wife, so that's what I'm doing. If you can cook and clean, I'd be right happy for you to join me.

The winters here are hard, but the mountains are beautiful. There's even a lake we can visit on hot summer days. Please say you'll be my wife. I've enclosed money for your train fare and for food along the way. I do hope you'll choose me to be your husband.

Sincerely,

David Jack Smith

Grace read over the letter once more, realizing there was something about David Jack Smith that was pulling at her heartstrings. He made no mention of parents, just of a sister. He sounded like he was alone in the world, and she wanted to take his hand and face the world at his side.

Looking up from the letter, she realized that all the chatter had stopped, and everyone was looking at her expectantly. This was the first letter she'd received since moving from the orphanage. She'd been there for five years, which felt like forever. "I'll want you to read the letter, Mrs. Durant, but I think I've found myself a husband."

Mrs. Durant smiled as she took the letter from Grace. "I think you have found your husband. We'll make sure all your clothes are repaired this weekend, and you can take a train out on Monday!"

Grace turned to Sadie, who was sitting at her side. "I have to go."

Sadie nodded, but her face seemed to be accusing. Grace knew they would need to have a long talk. Perhaps after supper.

After supper, she found a quiet spot in the parlor where she could talk to Sadie. "I should have told you the day I requested the ads. I'm so very sorry I didn't."

Sadie nodded. "I appreciate the apology, but why didn't you?"

"I wasn't sure how to tell you. We've been best friends for as long as either of us can remember, and I'm leaving you. I really will try to have my future husband find someone else for you to marry there!"

Sadie smiled, but a single tear betrayed her true feelings. "I don't want you to go, but I want you to be happy. You really will write every week?"

"Once I get there I will. He's all the way in Washington Territory. It's not going to be a short ride on the train." Grace sighed. "I've never been on a train. I always thought we'd take a trip together."

"I did too. Once we had enough money saved." Many of the girls had families they sent money to, but not Grace and Sadie. They had both squirreled away as much money as they could, knowing they would need it one day. Sadie smiled at her friend. "Just don't forget about me, even though you'll be far away, living the life of luxury as a new wife."

"I'm not certain it will be a life of luxury. He wants someone who can cook and clean."

"And you do both beautifully!" Sadie said. "I am happy for you. I'm just a little sad for me."

"Understandably. Do you want to help me make a dress this weekend? I plan to go to the mercantile as soon as they open in the morning for some fabric. The dress will serve as both my wedding dress and Sunday best."

"I would love to help you! If I can't be there for the wedding, then I definitely want to help with your dress for it!"

Grace hugged her friend close. "I wish I could just pack you in my suitcase and take you with me, but I have a feeling Mr. Smith won't want me to bring along a friend."

"I wish we could do that as well, but I'm counting on you to find me a husband!"

"That's the plan."

EARLY THE NEXT MORNING, Grace and Sadie headed to the store in town and looked at different fabrics. Sadie had a good eye for color, so she chose colors that would look good on her friend, and Grace chose her favorite.

They finally found a light blue fabric that would work beautifully. "Do you want to marry in blue?" Sadie asked.

"As long as I look my best, I don't care what color I marry in."

They purchased the fabric for the dress, some buttons, and thread before going back to the boarding house. When they arrived, they found Mrs. Durant in the parlor with Grace's clothes in front of her.

She was digging through everything, trying to find what needed to be mended.

"I was going to bring you the clothes that needed to be mended. You didn't have to get them yourself," Grace said.

Mrs. Durant smiled. "When you two said you were headed to the store this morning, I knew you were going to feel the need to make a dress for yourself. So, I took it upon myself to start the mending. The other girls plan to come down and help as soon as they finish their poetry reading upstairs."

Grace nodded. She hated to miss their poetry club, but not having a new dress to wear to her wedding would be much worse. "I hope I can get a couple of the girls to work on basting while others work on mending. I feel bad asking my friends to work for me during their time off, but I don't think we'll get finished if I don't."

Mrs. Durant laughed. "Don't you worry about that. The girls are all thrilled to see one more person get out of the factory and move on to doing something they will enjoy."

Grace was a little nervous about who she would find waiting for her in Clover Creek, but she still felt as if she was doing the right thing. She could only hope and pray that her future husband was as kind as he sounded in his letter.

Soon the other girls came down the stairs, two sitting to mend with Mrs. Durant, and the other two working on basting the pieces that had been cut out together.

"We should sing while we work!" Sadie suggested. All the girls loved poetry, but Sadie had a memory for lyrics and a beautiful voice.

Grace nodded, smiling. "I'd love to have one last sing along before I leave."

Sadie started an old favorite that could be sung in rounds, and the other girls started singing when their round started. The music was joyous and filled Grace's heart with hope for the future. One day soon, she would look back at this day as an important part of her send-off.

By the time supper was ready, all the mending had been done, and the dress was taking shape nicely. None of them wanted to work on the sabbath, so it was important they get it done just as quickly as they could.

At supper, there was the usual conversation, and everyone took the opportunity to tell Grace the one thing they loved best about her. Grace knew she would cherish the thoughts of the other girls forever.

After supper all the girls went into the parlor to work on Grace's dress while Mrs. Durant did the dishes. All the smaller pieces were sewn together, and now it was time to sew the pieces together to form the dress and hem it.

When the dress was finished, Grace stripped to her undergarments and pulled it over her head. Sadie buttoned up the back, while Cecilia and Audrey put pins in the dress where the hem should be. Sadie went to work on the sleeves of the dress.

Soon they were all putting the last little details on the dress. When Grace tried it on again, just before bedtime—well it was past bedtime, but right before they went to bed—it fit perfectly. "Thank you! I can't believe we did this in one day!" Grace was amazed at what the four of them could do together.

"Just leave it down here when you go to bed, and I'll get it all nice and pressed for you," Mrs. Durant said. "I've let you all stay up late, but we have church in the morning, so I expect lights out and all of you trying to sleep quickly!"

Grace looked at Mrs. Durant. "Thank you for pressing it for me. None of us got our baths tonight."

Mrs. Durant sighed. "Do the best you can with the water in your room, and we'll make sure everyone gets a bath tomorrow."

Grace stooped down and kissed the matron on the cheek. "Thank you for making our lives so much better with your kindness. I'll never forget you."

Mrs. Durant smiled. "You'll never be able to forget me. I plan to write to you often, and hopefully I can include letters from everyone else as well."

"That would be wonderful."

As she fell asleep that night, she couldn't help letting her mind drift to Jack Smith. She didn't know why, but she felt she should call him by his middle name not his first name. She knew he had all his teeth, but little else about him. How could she possibly marry a man she knew so little about?

Then she remembered how often he'd mentioned his sister, with whom he ate most of his meals. He was a family man. As an orphan with no family to speak of, the idea of marrying a family man was very enticing. Soon, she would marry the man.

As she imagined him, he became a tall handsome fellow with a ready smile, who would always take her hand and help her from a wagon or buggy, and who would feel the need to hire a maid to help around the house and with the cooking. Twas a beautiful thing to think about. She was marrying the man of her dreams.

Well, at least until she met him, he would be the man of her dreams.

Chapter Two

It took a full two weeks for the trip across the continent to the tiny town of Clover Creek, set off in the mountains of the Washington Territory. As they went through the area, and she knew they were close to her final destination, she watched out the window, more and more excited by the minute.

She'd used a portion of the money Jack had sent her to bathe in the last town where there was a long enough break to do so. Most of the train's stops were simple whistle stops, and they were only in the city long enough for passengers to board and disembark the train.

She had put her new dress on after her bath, and she felt she looked her best to meet the man she was going to marry and spend the rest of her life with.

As the train stopped, she couldn't believe how beautiful her surroundings were. She'd heard portions of the west were barren wastelands, but this...this was more beautiful than anything she'd seen in Massachusetts.

With all the snow about, it should have looked like a monotonous world, but instead, it was pure beauty. Jack had described the place beautifully.

She grabbed her carpet bag from the floor beside her feet and stood to leave the train. She had become friends with a seat companion, but the companion had stopped a few cities before. Now she was on her own, completely alone in a part of the country she'd never even seen.

Walking to the front of the train, she smiled and thanked the conductor, and then she took the steps down and off the train.

There was only one person waiting on the platform, so she approached him, hoping it was her future husband. "You're not David, are you?"

The man nodded slowly. "Everyone calls me Jack. David was my father's name."

Grace nodded slowly, waiting for him to tell her more about his father.

"Do you have a trunk?"

"Yes, I do." She put a hand over her eyes to shield the sun's reflection off the snow. "There it is!"

Jack obediently went to fetch the trunk, and he carried it to the back of the wagon before climbing up to drive. He looked down at her standing beside the wagon, waiting for him to help her up. "What are you doing? We're going straight to Pastor Scott."

Grace blushed and hurried up into the wagon seat. She had to be careful with her skirts, but that didn't matter too terribly much. She'd done it before. Wishing he'd been like her dream where he'd always helped her up into the wagon, she shook her head, and refused to worry about it. She could teach him manners if need be.

As they drove through town, he was quiet. Grace decided she couldn't bear another minute of silence, and asked, "Is the church far?"

He shook his head. "Nothing is terribly far in this tiny community. You'll be able to walk many places when it's warmer."

"So your farm isn't far from town?"

He shook his head. "Not far. My sister and her husband have land on the outskirts of town. He builds beautiful furniture and sells it to make a living."

"Does your sister have a name?"

"My older sister is Sarah. I also have a younger sister named Poppy."

"No brothers?" she asked. It seemed like a dream to her to have a family. She couldn't remember her parents, and really had no idea where she came from. Other than the orphanage of course.

"Okay, here's the whole family. Sarah is ten years older than I am. Then comes me. Charles is a year younger, and Poppy is two years younger."

"And your parents?"

"Both died on the trail coming west in 1852. Sarah had just turned eighteen when Pa died, and Sarah became our mom, whether she wanted to or not. She married right away so we would always be cared for."

"I can't wait to meet her. She sounds like a good person."

"Sarah's the best. She has six children of her own now, but I'm still invited for every meal. She bakes extra loaves of bread for Charles and me so we'll always have a good lunch, even if we don't make it to her and Elmer's house for a meal. But honestly? I've never been one to turn down a well-cooked meal. And Sarah is a wonderful cook."

Grace was glad he was offering information now, and she wasn't having to question him about everything. "Were you the first family to settle here?" she asked.

"No, not at all. Our wagon train was the first to settle here, however. A few families have come in since, but it's mostly been our company. We all gathered around and settled together. We had to!"

"And are you happy you all settled together?"

He nodded. "I am. I remember the trail fondly for the most part. There was always work to do, but we were outside every day and there was no school for a while."

She glanced over at him, admiring his profile. He had all his teeth as he'd said, but he was a relatively handsome man, with dark hair and green eyes. He would make a good husband. She just knew he would. "It sounds nice."

"What about you? What's your family like?"

She shrugged. "I was orphaned when I was three. I was raised in an orphanage and they found me a place to work when I turned fourteen. I've worked in a textile mill since then."

He looked at her in surprise for a moment. "How did you like the mill?"

"It was awful. It was always either too hot or too cold. We were packed into one room with no real space around us." She shook her head. "If it hadn't been for my dear friends and our poetry club, I wouldn't have lasted as long as I did."

"How old are you?" he asked.

"Nineteen. And I know I'll be working still, but it will be for my family and not for a stranger who underpays me and treats me as if I'm a machine."

"It sounds as if you've had a hard life."

"As have you. I can't imagine losing my parents that way." She frowned. "Well, I guess I did lose my parents, but I just don't remember doing it."

"Let's pray that our lives will be better from this day forward," he said.

He stopped in front of a small building and jumped down from the wagon. "Pastor Scott is waiting for us."

He went and stood beside the door to the church while she struggled to get down with no help. His sister must have raised him with no manners at all, but she was out of the mill. And men could be taught.

She hurried to join him at the door, and he opened it and went through first, allowing it to swing closed toward her. She caught the door, muttering under her breath at his lack of manners.

The church was beautiful. She walked toward the front with him, and stopped in front of a man in his late thirties or early forties. "Are you two ready to be married?" the pastor asked.

Grace nodded. "I'm ready."

"Me too!" Jack said.

The ceremony was quick, and when Jack was told to kiss her, he leaned down and brushed his lips across her cheek.

Grace felt as if she'd been rejected, but she said nothing as she followed him out of the church.

He was quiet again as he drove. Finally, she broke the silence. "You didn't want to kiss me?"

Jack turned red and rubbed the back of his neck. "I've never kissed a woman, and I just didn't want the first time to be in church with the pastor right there."

"I see. I've never been kissed by a man either."

"I guess we'll figure it out together!" He reached out and squeezed her hand, and it was all she needed to feel a great deal better about their situation. "I'm taking you to Sarah's for lunch. She wanted to do a family meal and get to know you as soon as you arrived. I hope you don't mind."

"Not at all. It'll be fun." At least Grace hoped it would. His sister sounded like a nice person, but you never could tell until you actually met someone.

He pulled into a yard of a house, which seemed to be attached to a store. After she got down, she asked, "So is that your brother-in-law's store?"

"He does his furniture building there, and he sells out of it as well. They tried when we first arrived for Sarah to deal with customers, but after the first set of twins was born, it became too much."

"First set of twins? There's more than one?"

"Three actually. Sarah seems to only have twins." He shrugged. "It's odd, but no one cares much. Doc Bentley just said that some women have twins."

"There's a doctor here?" she asked, getting excited.

"There is. He was on the trail with us."

She got down from the wagon again, carefully watching the skirt of her dress. For the first time in her life, she wished women could wear trousers so they wouldn't always have to be moving their skirts out of the way.

Just as her feet were on the ground, she heard a voice say, "David Jack Smith! Why aren't you helping your wife down from that wagon? You'd better start showing her some manners!"

Jack looked embarrassed but Grace was thrilled to hear the man had been taught manners, even if he wasn't displaying them. It should be easier than she'd thought to nudge him in the right direction.

Grace didn't say a word to Jack, instead she called out to Sarah. "Are you my new sister? I've never had a family, and I love the idea of a sister!"

Sarah laughed. "A much older sister."

"That's all right with me!" Grace headed toward the house with a bounce in her step. "Jack has told me so much about you, I feel like I already know you." Grace embraced the other woman.

Sarah smiled. "I can't wait to get to know you. Winters here are hard, but they're worth it."

"Thank you for having us for lunch today. I'm so glad I don't have to immediately cook a meal. Two weeks on a train, and I wasn't sure I'd be able to walk to get off the thing!"

"Well, come in! My four oldest are at school today. I have three sets of twins. I had twin boys, then twin girls, and my youngest are a boy and a girl."

"I hope I don't follow in your footsteps with the twins. I can't imagine giving birth to two every time."

Sarah patted her belly. "We're hoping for just one this time, but I seem to pop out twins for some reason." She motioned toward the table. "Sit down!"

Grace sat in the spot indicated, noting that the youngest twins were in highchairs and watching her with wide eyes. "Oh, their chairs are beautiful!"

"They are! My husband made them for the first two, and I've used them on the other two sets of twins." Sarah shook her head. "Elmer is supposed to join us for lunch, and so is Jack. I don't see either one of them."

"Is it possible Jack went to tell Elmer we're here for lunch?"

"It's possible. I didn't see where he went because I was focused on you." Sarah shrugged. "Charles should be here any minute, but Poppy didn't think it was a good idea for her to come. She's the schoolmarm, and she supervises the children at lunchtime."

"Well, of course, she couldn't come then. I look forward to meeting her."

"She was sad she couldn't be here to greet you. She still lives with us. I'm hoping a beau will keep her from teaching soon, but I'm not sure if that's what she wants. She loves teaching."

"It sounds delightful to me!" Grace sniffed the air. "I smell fresh bread...and what is that? Stew?"

"Yes, it's stew!" Sarah started serving bowls of the steaming concoction. "How long has it been since you had a hot meal?"

Grace shook her head. "Before I left Massachusetts so at least two weeks. They had sandwiches on the train, and I suppose I could have eaten in the dining car, but I wanted to save as much of Jack's money as I could."

The door opened to a young man stomping his feet, his eyes gravitating to Grace. "I'm Charles."

Grace smiled. "It's good to meet you, Charles. I'm Grace."

Charles tilted his head to one side, studying her. "I figured you'd look like an old crone. You're pretty!"

Grace couldn't help but laugh at that. "I'm sorry to spoil your expectations."

"Not at all. I won't mind looking at you like I thought I would."

Sarah shook her head. "Charles, go find Elmer and Jack. And no more talk about old crones. That was very rude of you."

Charles rushed out the door, and as soon as he was gone, both women burst into laughter, causing the twins to fake laugh. "Charles seems to be more outspoken than Jack."

Sarah nodded. "I bet you had a hard time getting Jack to talk at all, but Charles will say anything to anyone. He doesn't often think before he speaks."

"Is Charles married?" Grace asked, wondering if he wouldn't be the perfect husband for Sadie.

"He's not, but don't let your eye stray. It wouldn't be nice to pit the brothers against each other." Sarah's friendly manner changed abruptly.

"No! I am hoping to find a husband for my dear friend Sadie. It would be nice if we could be sisters. We've always thought of ourselves that way."

Sarah looked relieved. "Tell me about Sadie."

"We met when I first went to the orphanage. I don't remember meeting her, but Matron used to tell us that when I first arrived I would cry and cry. Sadie started sneaking into my bed every night to comfort me. We went to work at the mill together, and she's still there, but she doesn't want to be. The hardest part of coming here was saying goodbye to her."

"I see. Well, observe Charles for a bit before you bring up a wife for him. He'd jump at the chance, but he's something of a jokester. I'm not sure he's ready for marriage yet."

"I will."

The men came in together then. "Sorry, dear," said the only one Grace hadn't met yet, as he stomped his feet to get rid of the snow before coming inside. "I needed an extra set of hands for a minute, and Jack was there, so I put him to work helping me."

Sarah nodded. "I thought it was something like that." She set a loaf of fresh bread on the table and served each adult a bowl of stew. The twins were given a small portion of meat and a bit of carrots and potatoes.

As soon as Sarah sat down, the entire family bowed their heads and Elmer gave the blessing. It included thanks for Grace arriving safely, which made her quite pleased. It was odd how very welcome this family made her feel.

Chapter Three

After they'd finished the delicious meal Sarah had prepared, Jack and Grace headed to his house. When she walked in she was amazed at how very clean it was. She'd been certain a bachelor would have a messy home.

It was a nice two-story house. The kitchen, parlor, and dining room were on the first floor, and there were four bedrooms upstairs. A fireplace was in the parlor, and Grace could just imagine long romantic nights in front of the fire.

"All sheets are clean. Sarah and Poppy put some food into the cellar, so you'd have something to cook with. They even picked out some nice dishes for us." Jack watched her closely as she explored, expecting her to react negatively to something, but she seemed pleased with her new home.

"It's so clean! I expected I'd have to come here and clean up a year's worth of messes."

He grinned sheepishly, rubbing the back of his neck. "Sarah and Poppy did that for you."

"Oh, so I wasn't wrong about that then?" Grace's eyes twinkled with laughter. "Don't worry. I enjoy keeping house and cooking. We were all trained to do those things in the orphanage."

"Even the boys?" he asked, looking surprised.

"It was an all-girl's orphanage. But that meant we were taught to fix things that were broken. We all know how to milk a cow and mend a fence. And we all received an eighth-grade education whether we wanted to or not." Grace had loved learning, but many of the girls hated it. She left out the fact that she'd also learned to care for small children. She was certain he understood that.

"So you'll be able to help me when the barn needs fixing?" he asked.

"I would rather your brother helped you and not me," she told him softly.

"I can make that happen." He stood awkwardly with his hat in his hand. "I guess I should go and work. I only had time to do the milking and gather eggs before it was time to fetch you this morning."

"All right. What would you like for supper?" she asked, uncertain what he even enjoyed eating.

He shrugged. "There's a chicken in the cellar. Do whatever you want with it."

Her eyes widened. "A whole chicken? Just for us?"

"Make enough for supper and lunch tomorrow. Then it won't seem like you're making so much." He walked toward her, removed his hat, and set it on the dining room table. "Now, about that kiss that didn't feel right in front of Pastor Scott."

Grace was surprised to see him lower his head for a kiss, but she certainly wasn't unwilling. He was her husband after all. There should be kisses, and lots of them.

When his lips touched hers, Grace put one hand at the nape of his neck, and allowed him to kiss her. It didn't take long before she felt something inside her stirring. His kisses were nice, and she enjoyed them a great deal.

When he lifted his head, his eyes looked like they were glazed over. "I'll be home around six for supper," he said softly as he grabbed his hat and left the house, leaving Grace standing beside the table and staring at the closed door.

This man...Well, she had married well. If only she could get him to mind his manners.

Instead of starting to cook right away, because she had hours to go before supper needed to be done, Grace went upstairs, and looked at the bedrooms. She was certain the one at the top of the stairs was the one she would share with Jack. She walked to the bed, removed her shoes, and climbed under the covers, still fully clothed. She hadn't been allowed to sleep flat since she'd left Millshore, and she was tired. More tired than she'd ever been.

She promised herself she would wake in an hour so she could start supper and do a bit of baking.

When she woke, it was dark outside. She hurried down the stairs and glanced at the clock in the parlor. It was already four-thirty. She only had an hour and a half to put supper on the table.

Hurrying to open the cellar door, she went down the steep stairs and found the chicken. She spotted some carrots and green beans as well. Since she'd had carrots for lunch, she chose the green beans and took it upstairs along with the chicken.

She found flour in a cabinet in the kitchen, and she immediately put the chicken on to boil. She'd make chicken and dumplings for him. It was one of her favorite meals.

She dropped the dumplings just fifteen minutes before suppertime, but she knew they would cook quickly and be ready on time. She had the green beans simmering in a pot already, and she'd just need to serve the meal.

There was a bucket of milk on the counter, and she decided he must drink milk with some meals, so that's what she poured into two glasses for them.

Jack walked in a few minutes after six. "Something smells wonderful."

"Chicken and dumplings," she called back.

"That's not something I've ever eaten," he said, walking into the kitchen to join her at the stove.

"Wash your hands and face, and it will be ready."

Jack didn't argue, instead going to the pitcher and bowl there in the kitchen and using it to wash his hands and face. "I'm clean now. Can we eat?"

Grace laughed. "Yes, we can eat." She served up two bowls of chicken and dumplings and carried them to the table. Then she carried the milk over.

Jack sat down at the head of the table, and she looked at the foot of the table and frowned. Instead she took the seat closest to him.

After their prayer, she watched him as he took a bite of the chicken and dumplings. He smiled and nodded, waving a hand in front of his mouth. "I need to wait until it's a bit cooler, but this is delicious. You can make this every day if you'd like."

"It's my favorite meal. I was hoping you'd like it as much as I do."

"I do. I very much do."

"What did you do this afternoon?" she asked.

He shrugged. "I made sure the cows had access to water, and I spilled some salt around the barn so I wouldn't keep slipping on the ice. My cat had kittens. I probably need to stop calling her Tom now."

"You have a cat?" Grace had never had a pet. They hadn't been allowed in the orphanage or in the boarding house.

"A barn cat. Good mouser."

"Can I have one of the kittens when they're old enough? Please?"

He frowned. "Pets are a lot of work."

She sighed. "I've never been able to have a pet. They weren't allowed in the orphanage or in the boarding house where I've lived since leaving the orphanage."

He looked at her and shook his head. "You can have your pick of the kittens."

Grace clapped her hands together. "Oh, thank you, Jack. I want one more than anything else."

"There are three. One is black, one is a gray tabby, and the other is calico. You choose the one you want, and I'll make sure you get it."

"Can we go see them after supper?"

He nodded. "Sure. They're in a corner of the barn."

"Are they too cold out there?" she asked.

"No, they should be fine. They are all lying in a pile beside their mother."

"Oh, I can't wait to see them!" She found herself picking at her chicken and dumplings because she was so excited to see the kittens.

When Jack asked for a second helping, she wanted to tell him no, but that wouldn't be at all right. He'd worked out in the cold all day while she'd napped upstairs in his bed—their bed.

She got him another large helping of the chicken and dumplings, and only then did she see the beans. They were ready, and she only had to serve them.

She found small plates and served the beans and took them to him. "I was so excited to have chicken and dumplings, I almost forgot the green beans."

"Having tasted the main course, I'd have forgotten the green beans as well."

When he finally sat back in his chair and patted his belly, she took that as an indicator that he was finished with the meal. She cleared the table and poured the water she had boiling into the basin and dropped the dishes into it.

Then she grabbed her coat and pulled it on, buttoning it up. "Let's go see the kitties!"

"You are obsessed with the kittens."

"I've never had a pet," she reminded him softly.

"Let's go see them then." He opened the door for her and waited for her to go through it before following. "I'm sorry I wasn't using manners before. I wasn't sure if you'd want me taking your hand every time you got into or out of the wagon."

She shook her head. "I like it when you touch me."

Suddenly all Jack could think about was their wedding night. He wondered if it would be inappropriate to tell her to skip the dishes and just go to bed with him, but he decided against it. Instead, he'd wait until she was finished before making her go up the stairs with him.

When she saw the kittens, Grace knelt in the straw, and stroked one of their tiny heads. Tom looked at her for a moment, but she must have decided Grace wasn't a threat. "Can I pick one up?" she asked.

"I think Tom would hide them if we tried. We'll wait a week or two, and then you can. Come out and pet them as often as you'd like so you can choose your favorite."

Grace kept stroking little noses, but finally she stood. "I'm coming back out tomorrow and I'll bring Tom a bowl of milk. She needs milk to feed her babies."

"I give her milk every day, but if you want to give her more, that's fine with me. Milk is something we're not short of here. This is a dairy farm after all."

"I thought you grew crops. I didn't know you were a dairy farmer."

Jack smiled at her, offering a hand to help her up. "I think there are many things we have yet to learn about one another."

She stood right next to him, smiling. "I think you may be right." Standing on tiptoe, she kissed his cheek, and they started for the house. "I need to do the dishes as soon as we get inside."

He nodded. "I'll be in the parlor when you're done." He wanted to say he'd be waiting for her in bed, but he had a feeling she wouldn't like that much.

They both removed their coats, and he removed his hat. "It's not terribly smart going out at night here. The temperature is much colder than during the day due to the high altitude."

"I'll try to remember to visit my little friends during the day then."

He grinned. "Tomorrow after my chores, I'm going to do a little hunting. It would be nice to have some fresh meat around here."

"We had chicken for supper! At the orphanage, we only ate meat twice a week. It was too expensive to do otherwise."

He shook his head. "I prefer to have meat every day, for every meal even. If I can get a deer or elk tomorrow, we'll have meat to share with family, and we'll eat well for a while. All of the men in my family take turns hunting, and we share what we get."

"Elmer doesn't strike me as a hunter."

"Oh, he prefers not to hunt, but he takes his turn. He doesn't think the rest of us should have to feed his family, even though he fed and clothed us for years. I wish I could talk him into letting Charles and I handle it." He put his hands at her waist and pulled her to him for a kiss. "Get the dishes done, then join me in the parlor."

Grace nodded. His kisses made her weak in the knees, but she wasn't quite ready for him to know that. She hurried into the kitchen and washed she supper dishes, putting everything where she'd found it. Some of the organization in the kitchen didn't make much sense to her, so she would work on rearranging things. But first, she needed to do her laundry. Two weeks on a train, and everything she owned was filthy.

When the kitchen was as clean as she'd found it, she went into the parlor and sat on the sofa beside him. Not too close, but definitely close enough it wouldn't seem as if she didn't want him to touch her.

He was reading a book which surprised her. She'd been told that only lazy women read in the orphanage, and that men never read books. Apparently, Matron hadn't known all she thought she did.

"What are you reading?" she asked softly.

He smiled. "Farmer's Almanac. It might not seem terribly interesting, but it helps me know what the weather coming up will look like."

"Ahh."

"Do you like to read?" he asked.

"I'm afraid to answer that. I was taught that only lazy women read, but I love to read. So I won't tell you I love to read, for fear you'll think I'm lazy."

He laughed at her logic. "I see. I think."

"I have some poetry books in my trunk, and I read them when I have a free minute or two. The girls in the boarding house and I all had a little poetry club where we'd share what we'd read or our own works. It was fun."

"I have no problem with you reading. It doesn't make you lazy. It makes you smarter."

"Do you really think so?" she asked.

He nodded emphatically. "I do think so." He leaned over to kiss her again. "I think I like kissing you as well."

She smiled. "I think I could get used to that."

"Good! You're going to need to."

Chapter Four

Grace rose before the sun was up the following morning and dressed quickly in the dark. She had put an old dress into her trunk that she hadn't planned to wear except on laundry days, and this was a day of laundry.

She went downstairs and put on her coat, going to the chicken house to collect the eggs for their breakfast. And for a cake. She wanted to make a cake for him that day. He was such a pleasant man, she found herself wanting to do many things for him.

Hurrying back inside, she started breakfast, making a casserole from eggs and bacon and leftover bread. As she used the leftover bread, she reminded herself that she needed to bake some bread that day as well.

By the time Jack came down the stairs, Grace had their breakfast ready. "You should have woken me so I could get the milking done before breakfast."

"You seemed tired, so I let you sleep. I gathered the eggs, but didn't do any of the milking. I'll put on a coat and help you milk if you'd like."

He shook his head. "No, I've been milking my entire life, and I know exactly how I like it done. You would mess up my system."

She smiled at that. "I found coffee in the cabinet, so I made some. Are you a coffee drinker?"

He nodded. "Especially on cold winter mornings when I need to be out milking cows and doing some hunting."

"Well, let me pour you a cup then. Cream or sugar?"

He shook his head. "No, I take it black."

"I'll remember that." She sat down at the table with him and after they'd prayed over the meal, she took a bite of the casserole she'd made.

They'd had something similar at the orphanage, but there had been no bacon to waste on the meal.

He took a bite and smiled. "This is really good!"

"Thank you! We used to have it at the orphanage, but I remembered you want meat with every meal so I added bacon to this."

"I like it. Very much."

"I'll remember that. Do you like pancakes? Or johnny cakes?"

He chuckled. "I can't believe you know about johnny cakes. I thought they were a delicacy of the trail."

"We had them often at the orphanage. I haven't had them since, but I love the simple flavor of them."

"So do I. Sarah made them for us on the trail."

"How far were you from your destination when your father died?"

He frowned. "We were a day or two away from Oregon City. She married Elmer right after Pa died, and I'm glad she did. Elmer was very much like a father to me."

"I'm glad you had someone looking after you."

"My mother was one of the first deaths, but Doc Bentley said they both died of cholera. Pa wouldn't drink coffee late in the day, and Ma wouldn't drink it at all. She wouldn't even drink tea. She always said water was what she preferred, and she'd have what she liked while on a two-thousand-mile walk." He shook his head. "Sarah made sure the rest of us drank coffee and only coffee."

"It sounds like Sarah was smart. Was it hard for you to obey her?"

He shook his head. "No, because I grew up obeying her. She was ten years older, and she was the one taking care of me often."

"Was it hard for you to think of her as a sister and then a mother?"

"Sarah was always just my sister. I never thought of her as my mother. Poppy did for a while, but she was only six when Ma and Pa died."

Grace stood to clear the table. "Will you be home for the noon meal?"

Jack nodded. "I will."

"Would you mind having chicken and dumplings again?"

"I would enjoy that a great deal." Jack stood up and kissed Grace's cheek. "The milk wagon will be here soon. I need to get to work!"

"Have a good day!" she called as he walked toward the door, donning his coat and hat and leaving.

As soon as he was gone, she hurried upstairs to get her dirty clothes to wash. It didn't feel right to let him see her unmentionables, so she would do the laundry while he was gone.

After hanging the clothes in the cellar, she started the bread for the day. She planned to make two loaves per day and see if it was enough. She had a feeling he was going to be a big eater.

While she was working, she hummed a song that had been one of Sadie's favorites. She promised herself she would write both Sadie and Mrs. Durant before going to bed that night. She'd work on letters to Rebecca and Josephine the next day, and the other girls at the boarding house after that. She didn't particularly like writing letters, but she did love receiving them.

When Jack came back for lunch, he pointed to a tree he had an elk hanging upside down in. "I'll carve it for you, but you need to share with Sarah."

"I will. Happily!" His hands had blood on them, and this time she didn't have to remind him to wash his hands and face. He did both automatically.

He sat down at the table with a smile on his face. "I'm excited to eat your chicken and dumplings again."

She laughed. "I like them so much, you will be sick of them soon."

"I don't know if that's even possible."

"I certainly hope it's not!"

After their prayer, she asked, "What do you have planned for this afternoon?"

"I need to mend some stalls in the barn. The cows mostly stay inside in the winter, but I let them out on warm days. Today is not warm, and one of the cows managed to kick some of the boards off her stall. It's harder to mend things with the cows right there, but I'll make it work."

"Do you need help?" she asked.

He shook his head. "No, you stay and do all the womanly things that need done. If I run into trouble, I'll get Charles to help me."

"Sounds good." She didn't really want to go out and help in the barn, but she needed him to know she would anytime he needed her to. "Would it be all right if I bought fabric for curtains with the money I have left from what you sent to me?"

He smiled. "Absolutely. I would love it if you did that. I'm surprised you had anything left."

"I'm a very frugal woman. I grew up in an orphanage and never wore a new dress until I was living in the boarding house. I saved almost every penny I made."

"Really?" He seemed genuinely surprised.

"Really. I brought the money with me inside a sock under other things in my trunk. It's not a fortune, but it's a good amount considering what I was paid."

Jack smiled. "I never thought I'd have a frugal wife, but here you are." He drank the last of his coffee. "I think Elmer would love it if you went to Sarah's and taught her to be frugal as well."

Grace laughed. "Elmer might love it, but I have a feeling Sarah wouldn't."

"Probably not." He stood. "Thank you for lunch. It was delicious." With a kiss on her cheek, he put on his winter clothes and left.

While he was gone, she went to the cellar to see if she could find something for supper. She didn't know how long it would be before the meat was ready, so she wanted to make other plans.

She found more bacon, but no other meat. So she thought about what she could make with bacon. Finally she decided to make baked potatoes and she would cook the bacon, cutting it into tiny pieces to go on the potatoes. She made four potatoes, thinking he would eat three and she could have the fourth.

She brought up her wash and ironed it. She hadn't done laundry in a long while, but she certainly remembered how to do it.

She promised herself she would go into town to buy fabric the next day. It would be fun to see a little more of the town. She hoped that Jack wouldn't mind her using his wagon.

She sat down to write her letters after punching down the bread dough. They were going to have fresh bread with their supper, and she was excited. There was a ball of butter in the cellar, and she'd cut off a piece to use.

Her mind was on supper, but she forced herself to write to Sadie first, telling her that Jack had a brother who seemed nice, but she would scout the church congregation on Sunday to make sure he was the best potential groom for her friend.

Her letter to Mrs. Durant was more of a thank you note than anything else. She was so happy to be able to get up in the morning and choose the chores she would do that day. She didn't have to worry about her arms and shoulders aching from hours and hours in front of a loom.

She didn't love Jack. Well, not yet anyway, but she felt she could love him, which is what mattered more to her than anything else.

By the time Jack was home for the evening, she had both letters written and addressed, wanting to mail them when she purchased fabric the following day.

She pulled the potatoes from the oven and crumbled up the bacon, explaining to Jack what she was doing with it. He nodded. "That sounds delicious."

"It does to me too! I've never had it that way, but we often had baked potatoes for meals at the orphanage. I made one for me and three for you. I hope that's enough."

"If all three are this big, it should be plenty."

"I made fresh bread as well. And a cake. I thought you might like dessert."

Jack grinned. "Are you trying to spoil me?"

"Isn't that what the wife is supposed to do?"

"Well, sure, I guess. Sarah doesn't spoil Elmer too often." He pursed his lips thinking about it. "You know? She does. She makes cakes all the time. I thought they were for me and my siblings, but I think they were for Elmer. Maybe she does spoil him."

"You work hard all day. I don't have to sit in front of a loom anymore, and my shoulders don't ache nearly as much as they did. I want to spoil you as much as I can."

"All right," he said, kissing her softly. "I'm glad you don't have to sit at a loom anymore either. I know it's what you had to do, but I never want you to have to work outside our home again."

"What about when I want to put in a kitchen garden."

He shook his head. "You know that's not what I meant."

"Wash up and I'll get supper on the table."

He was more than pleased with the meal. "The bacon with this was a stroke of genius."

"Thank you. Could I make a roast from the elk meat tomorrow night?" she asked.

"Of course."

"And I want to borrow the wagon if I may. I need to go to pick out fabric and send two letters to Massachusetts. They'll worry about me until they know I'm safe."

"After the milking I'll take you. We'll go in the sleigh because it looks like we're getting lots of snow tonight."

"I've never ridden in a sleigh!"

"You'll love it," he said with a grin. "Elmer made mine, and it's fast. Have you been sledding?"

She shook her head. "The orphanage wouldn't let us do anything that could possibly hurt us. They didn't want the doctor bills."

"That's sad. We'll go up the hill and sled down someday soon. I have some friends who live on the hill, and they'd be happy to meet you."

She clapped her hands in front of her. "I think that sounds positively wonderful. I've seen children sled, and it looks like so much fun!"

"Trust me. It is. It's my favorite thing about winter here. My work is harder in the winter, but sledding makes it all worthwhile."

"Did you always want to be a farmer?"

"My pa wanted to come west to be a rancher. When he died, I swore I'd ranch one day, but I realized quickly that I would prefer to run a dairy farm. I learned to make furniture with Elmer, but I don't have his knack for it or his love of wood. I'm much happier farming."

"Then that's what you should do. I don't care what you do, as long as we can make a living."

"Do you want children?" he asked, seemingly out of the blue.

She nodded slowly. "I do. I always dreamed I'd have a houseful of children. That was one thing that was good about the orphanage. There were always children to play with."

"Good. I want an even dozen I think."

She gaped at him for a moment. "All right. That's only four children to a room. We can make that work."

"Did you go see the kittens today?"

She shook her head. "No, I was too busy, and I forgot."

"We'll go right after supper then."

"You don't mind?"

"Not at all." Jack smiled at her. "You seem very happy when you're petting the kittens, and I like to see your pretty smile."

She blushed and looked at her plate for a moment. "I want to get to know the other men in this region. I want my friend Sadie to marry someone here so we can remain friends."

"I don't like the idea of you getting to know men, but tell me about this Sadie."

"I met her at the orphanage. I've been told she crawled in bed with me every night to get me to stop crying when I first arrived. We grew up together, and we both worked at the mill together, and we even shared a room in the boarding house. I feel like I've lost a sister without her by my side."

"Maybe Charles would marry her. Is she as pretty as you?"

"She's much prettier. You'll see."

"Then I'm sure Charles would happily marry her. I'll talk to him and see if he wants to hear more about her."

"Thank you," she said, standing to clear the table and get the dishes in the hot water before going out to see the kittens.

"Do you have a favorite kitten yet? I think the gray tabby would be good to have around."

Grace nodded. "I just want to see which one I'm most drawn to. I'll figure it out soon."

Chapter Five

Jack took Grace into town the next morning as soon as the milking was done. She mailed her letters and found blue gingham fabric to turn into curtains for the kitchen. She was only going to buy and make curtains for one room at a time. She really wasn't a fan of sewing, though she was very good at it.

Jack talked casually to the man behind the counter, while Grace found the things she needed not only for curtains, but also a few other kitchen essentials. There had only been enough flour for one day's baking, and she needed to make fresh bread daily. And they were almost out of sugar.

She felt a bit of guilt for everything she put on the counter to purchase, and she thought and rethought every single purchase. When she had everything on the counter, she took the money she needed from her reticule, paying the man behind the counter.

Jack watched in disbelief as she paid for everything. Did she think he was a pauper? He'd have to talk to her about their financial situation someday very soon. He wasn't like a dirt farmer, who earned money once a year. He had a contract with a dairy not too far away. and he brought in money every week. She needn't continue to embarrass him by paying for all of her purchases on her own.

He carried all of their supplies to the sleigh for her, but he had to make two trips with the amount of flour and sugar she'd gotten. When they were both tucked neatly into the sleigh under thick, warm blankets, he started the drive toward home.

"What you did back there embarrassed me a great deal," he said softly.

"What did I do?" Grace looked at him in confusion.

"You paid for everything yourself. I have an account at the store I settle every month, and I had cash in my pocket to pay for the meal. Why did you pay yourself?"

Grace sighed. "I'm used to having to pay for things myself. I thought you wouldn't mind because we talked about how little I spend, and I told you I had money."

"Well, I do mind! If you go to the store without me, then I want you to put whatever you purchase on my account. If you are with me, I'll deal with the money, not you."

"I see." Grace said nothing else as she watched the landscape race by her. She was used to being independent after working so many hours at the factory. Now she was expected to let him handle all of their money? As far as she was concerned, she was as capable of taking care of their money as he was.

"What are we having for lunch?" he asked, when he realized she wasn't going to say anything else. She should have at least apologized, but she didn't bother.

"We have one meal left of the chicken and dumplings. I've been keeping it in the cellar, so it should still be good."

"That sounds delicious," he said. When he pulled the sleigh into their yard, she jumped down on her own, not wanting him to even touch her with the way he'd talked to her. She had a right to pay for things!

She went in and let him deal with the purchases while she started their lunch. She didn't even need to have chicken and dumplings hot, but she would do it to please him. Everything was about pleasing him. Why wasn't he concerned about pleasing her?

After bringing her purchases in and dumping them on the small table in the kitchen, Jack sat at the dining room table, waiting for her to get the meal on the table. He was still angry that she hadn't apologized to him for embarrassing him. Perhaps he should talk to Elmer about her, and get some good advice on getting your wife to be obedient.

Surely, Elmer had some tips because he knew his sister listened to her husband.

When Grace brought the food in, he wanted to say something about how much of his workday she'd wasted, but he decided it was uncalled for. Even if he was angry with her about something else, he needed to treat her kindly. That was what Elmer had told him before she'd come out to marry him. He'd given a lot of good advice about being a husband, but that's what stuck with Jack the most.

He said the prayer over their meal, and then they ate in silence. She had nothing to say to a man who didn't think she could use her own money to purchase things she wanted.

At the end of the very tense meal, he stood. "Thanks for fixing me lunch. I'll have a roast in to you in an hour or so."

"Thank you," she said softly, not really wanting to talk to him. What could she say now that she'd realized he was a man she could never live with happily?

Cleaning up the dishes after lunch took no time at all. She went to work on putting all of her purchases away, and then she set about reorganizing the kitchen so it was more to her liking. The job was labor intensive, but that was what she needed to stop being angry with Jack. If she could stop being angry with Jack. She still wasn't certain if she could even do it.

When he brought the meat in, she seasoned it then added onions, carrots, and potatoes. It would be the perfect supper. Even if she wasn't married to a perfect man. Then she formed the dough she'd made that morning into loaves of bread and stuck them in the oven. She couldn't not feed him just because she was upset with his behavior.

While the meat was cooking, she put on her coat and went out to visit the kittens. She sat on the ground with Tom and all three babies, stroking each one softly. Tom simply watched Grace as she moved her hand softly over each kitten. Then she reached out to pet Tom. "You're such a good mama, Tom. I hope I'm half as good as you are. Don't you think it's too cold out here with the babies though? Do you want to come into the house?"

Grace looked at the cats for another minute before making a decision. Perhaps Jack would make financial decisions, but she could make decisions about the house. She had to clean it, so if one of the cats made a mess, it would be her responsibility.

She stood up and went into the house, looking at the empty crate that her purchases had come in. She found a blanket upstairs, and she put the blanket into the box, making a nice little next for it.

Then she carried the box outside to the barn. First, she carefully put Tom in the box. Tom looked at Grace like she'd lost her mind, but she was obviously too tired to care much. And then Grace put the three babies into the crate with their mother.

She carried the box into the house, and set it in the kitchen. They'd stay warm there, because the stove was almost always going.

Once placed on the floor, Tom stood and looked around her. She must have found the relocation to her satisfaction, because she laid down with the kittens and promptly went to sleep, while they began nursing.

Grace glanced at the crate often as she finished making supper. Tom got out and explored a bit, but she went right back into the crate with her babies.

While she was mashing the potatoes that had cooked with the roast, Jack came in. "Cows have had their second milking of the day, but I couldn't find Tom and her babies. Any idea where they are?" He washed his hands and face at the basin.

Grace simply pointed at the crate and continued mashing the potatoes, trying to get their meal ready and not be upset with him, all at the same time.

Jack frowned. "I told you I didn't want them in the house."

"They were too cold outside. They needed to be indoors."

Jack sighed. "You have to be the most disobedient wife this side of the Mississippi."

"And you have to be the most overbearing bossy husband." She carried the bowl of mashed potatoes to the table without even looking at him.

The roast was on a platter, and the carrots were in another bowl. Carrying both into the dining room, she set them down and went back for the bread and butter.

Jack was standing in the kitchen gaping at her, as if he expected her to apologize for what she'd said, but she wouldn't. She'd been independent for too long to deal with his ridiculousness.

After everything else was on the table, she poured them each a glass of milk, which she set on the table. "Dinner's ready!" she called out.

Jack walked in, and bowed his head in prayer. This prayer made Grace ready to scream. "Dear Heavenly Father, we thank you for this food you have provided. Please help Grace to understand that it is my place to give orders and her place to obey them. In Christ's name we pray. Amen."

Grace stiffened her spine and served herself. The meal was delicious, and she was very happy it had turned out so well. But she wasn't going to talk to her ridiculous oaf of a husband. He wasn't worth wasting her words on.

Jack watched Grace as she ate her meal, expecting an apology for both her behavior and words. He was sure his prayer would have sent her the message she needed to hear so she could understand what he and God expected of her.

He ate three helpings of the delicious meal, all the while expecting her to apologize at any moment. When she didn't, he finished his meal and stormed away from the table. But he didn't touch the cats. She'd understand soon enough why he hadn't wanted them in the house.

Grace let Tom outside as she was doing the dishes. And by the time she was finished, Tom was ready to come back inside, scratching softly at the door.

Tom looked at Grace, and Grace gave her a bowl of milk, which she lapped up quickly before she returned to her babies. Grace smiled. "I do hope one day, I'll be as good of a mother as you are, Tom."

As soon as she was done in the kitchen, Grace went upstairs and pulled one of her poetry books from her trunk. Hopefully she would have a bit of time to read it before Jack came up.

And he could forget about his husbandly rights until he'd apologized to her for his actions. She'd come all this way not to be his indentured servant, but to be his partner in life. There was no way she would give up the freedom she'd found since quitting her job at the factory.

She'd put her book away and fallen asleep before Jack joined her in bed. He looked at her for a moment to determine if she was really sleeping, but then he undressed and joined her in bed. She'd been awfully prickly that day. He had to wonder if it was her time of the month that had made her behave so badly, but he wasn't about to ask. Elmer had told him that was never a question you asked a wife when she was acting a bit odd. But he was certain that was what her problem was.

She was sleeping on her side, facing the wall, so he did the same on the other side of the bed. If she couldn't understand why her behavior was wrong, then he truly didn't need her in his life.

Before he fell asleep, he promised himself he'd go to Elmer and have a talk about how to deal with a disobedient wife. There had to be a way.

AS SOON AS MILKING was done the following day, Jack headed to his sister's house to talk with Elmer. He needed every bit of advice he could get. There were four cats living in his house, and his wife only spoke when absolutely necessary.

At least Grace was still feeding him. He could say that much for his marriage.

When he arrived at his sister's he went straight to Elmer's workshop. Elmer was working on a dresser, and he immediately started telling Jack what help he needed. Jack didn't mind because he'd expected as much.

While Jack held something exactly where it needed to be, he started talking. "I need some advice from someone who has been married for a long time."

Elmer had a half-grin on his face. "Trouble in paradise? Already?"

Jack sighed. "She doesn't think she should have to do what I tell her. She's not speaking to me more than necessary because I told her I wanted to be the one to pay the shopkeeper when we went to town. How ridiculous is that?"

Elmer looked confused. "All the money is shared by the two of you, correct?"

"Yes, correct. Of course. I would never not let my wife have the money she needs for something."

"So when she paid, she paid with your money?"

"Yes, but I should have been the one handing the money to the shopkeeper. I was very embarrassed when she pulled money from her reticule and paid."

Elmer shook his head. "You're being ridiculous. No wife is going to do everything you say without complaint. And this thing? Why are you upset that she paid with your money?"

"It was money she earned from her job in the factory!" Jack was certain his brother-in-law would understand now.

"That doesn't matter, does it?"

"She hated that factory. And she saved almost every penny she made. I don't think she should spend the money she made working there on things for my house. She paid for fabric and flour and sugar, and many other things."

"What should she do with the money she earned? Do you want her to burn it?"

"Of course not! She worked too hard for it!"

Elmer shook his head. "You're not thinking logically. She worked there for years, and she now has money. That money should be spent. If she gave you the money, and you gave it back to her to spend, would that make you any happier?"

Jack frowned. "Of course not. But she was mad enough that I told her she needs to be obedient that she brought cats into my house! Tom had three babies."

"And you're still calling her Tom?"

"That's not the point! She shouldn't have brought kittens into my home without my permission."

"Your home? You don't share it with your wife?"

"Of course I do. Whatever I have is hers."

Elmer looked at Jack as if he was just a bit slow. "Then why are you upset that she brought cats into her home?"

"Because I told her not to! I'm the man of the house, and she needs to listen to me."

"What needs to happen is you need to be more sensitive to your wife's needs. She's not a child. She's been working for years. Show her some consideration."

Chapter Six

Grace was still angry when she woke up, and she wished she had a friend she could talk to who wasn't related to Jack. Jack's family had been wonderful, but who could she go to for marital advice other than Sarah?

She did her baking for the day, and shortly after she finished the lunch dishes, she set out to Sarah's house. It shouldn't take too terribly long to get there if she went through the snow instead of going along the road.

It took a lot more work to break the trail through the snow than she'd expected, and she arrived at Sarah's soaked and shivering.

Sarah pulled her inside. "Go to the fire. Where are your mittens?"

Grace's teeth were chattering as she answered. "It was a short walk. I didn't think I'd need them."

"It's never a short walk when you're breaking a trail in the snow! Coffee or tea?"

"Tea," Grace responded. She looked around and realized the twins weren't there. "Where are the babies?"

"They're down for their nap. I'm glad you came. I want to invite you to have tea tomorrow afternoon with my family. Tomorrow's Saturday, so all the children will be home as well as Poppy. She so wants to meet you."

Grace smiled. "That sounds lovely." Finally warm enough, she moved away from the stove. "Can I help in any way?"

"No, you just sit there and be warm for a minute or two. What brings you by?"

"Your brother is very opinionated about how I should act, and he's making me want to scream. How can I convince him that I can be a loving wife, even if I don't do every little thing he says."

Sarah brought their tea and sat down beside Grace. "What did he tell you to do?"

"He told me I can never pay for anything with my own money. He wants me to either use his account at the store or let him pay. Period." Grace felt herself getting all riled up again. "It makes no sense! I've worked for years, and I have money saved. I spent as little as I could. So what am I now supposed to do with that money? Burn it? Bury it like it's a treasure and hope someone finds it someday?"

Sarah smiled. "He would probably prefer that. My brother is a stubborn goose, and he doesn't deserve a wife as sweet as you."

"And because I was angry with him, I brought four cats into the house. Tom had babies, you see, and I've never had a pet."

"And I'm sure Jack told you not to bring cats into the house because he doesn't think cats are good for anything but catching mice."

"Well, he told me I could have one kitten, but I couldn't let any of them stay in the barn when it's so cold, so I brought them inside."

Sarah smiled. "It's your house as well as his. I think he needs to learn that he doesn't get to treat you like a maid or a guest because you're his wife. Keep working on him. Thankfully I never had to go through all that with Elmer. We were just thankful to still be alive at the end of each day."

"Now I feel terrible!" Grace said. "You were walking the Oregon Trail in your early marriage, and you made it through that. We're just fighting over little things."

"Trust me, Grace. It's all a bunch of little things that you have to figure out together. I wanted to start a ranch, but Elmer wanted to make furniture. The boys wanted to ranch as well, but they were young when they realized they could never sell or butcher a cow they'd named Anabelle."

Grace laughed. "I guess being dairy farmers suits them."

"It does. And they spend a lot of time helping out Elmer when he needs it. They're good boys."

"I need to learn to look for the good in him so that the little things don't bother me so much."

Sarah smiled, nodding. "We all need to do that with those we love. We know all their faults because we spend so much time together, but sometimes it's hard to remember to look for their good qualities."

"I'm going to do better at that starting right this minute!" Grace stood. "Thank you for the tea and conversation. I'm happy that you're my new sister." Grace put her coat back on, but Sarah shook her head.

"I'm going to have Elmer drive you home. There's no reason for you to be that cold going home. You'll catch your death!"

"I would appreciate it. I did make a path that I could walk back in though."

"When was the last time you looked outside?"

Grace turned to look out the window, and frowned. "It wasn't even snowing when I arrived."

"The storms here can be brutal. This one isn't a blizzard, but it did cover up the trail you made. Give me a minute." Sarah hurried away and came back with a confused looking Elmer.

When he saw Grace, he smiled, as if he knew some secret. "I'll hitch up the horse. I have a new standing sleigh that will be perfect for a trip across the field. I've been trying to find a reason to give it a try."

"Are you certain it's safe?" Sarah asked.

"As certain as I can be!"

A short while later, Grace was standing beside Elmer in the strangest looking contraption she'd ever seen. "What made you build this?"

Elmer grinned at her. "Some trips are so short, there's no point sitting down because you have to get right back up. I thought this would be nice for those times." He picked up the leads and the horse started moving swiftly toward her home. "Hold on tight!"

Grace almost fell but she grabbed on to the little handle he'd made on the sleigh, and held on for dear life. It only took a couple of minutes to get across the field, but it was the longest two minutes of her life.

Elmer was beside her, laughing like a loon. He was obviously pleased that his sleigh worked. Grace was happy when he stopped and she could get off. "I think I'll stick to boring sleighs in the future."

Elmer grinned at her, raising a hand in farewell. "Have fun!"

He drove the sleigh even faster toward his house. He disappeared almost immediately behind the heavy snow that was falling.

She went inside the house, took off her coat and sat down. Her knees were week, and despite the cold, she was certain her cheeks were white with the fear that sleigh had caused her. Never again would she agree to ride in his standing sleigh. It didn't feel safe at all.

After she'd warmed herself a bit, she walked into the kitchen to find another roast waiting for her on the counter. After a moment of indecision, she chopped it into small pieces, unsure if she'd make it into a stew or a soup. Either way, it would feel good to eat it after such a cold day.

She went down to the cellar and grabbed a few things that she would use. It would either be a stew or a soup or a combination thereof she decided.

She chopped up onions, carrots, potatoes, and green beans. All went straight into the pot with the pieces of meat. She would cook them with water, and then she'd make a roux and add it to the water. She only wished they had some barley, but she certainly wasn't going to ask Elmer for another ride to get anything. The man scared her.

She spent a little while with the kittens, getting a bowl of milk for Tom, and letting her out for a bit. Grace found that she was most drawn toward the little black kitten, They still looked like they were drowned mice, but the black one seemed to have more personality than the others.

Tom was back, and Grace was serving supper when Jack came in, stomping his feet. "I'm glad you didn't go anywhere in that snow today. I'd have worried about you."

The simple words were all Grace needed to hear. She put the bowls of stew down and ran to him, throwing her arms around him. "Let's not fight anymore."

"Does this mean you're going to be obedient?" he asked.

Grace smiled sweetly. "Let's not fight." Then she turned back to the kitchen, mumbling under her breath that he was crazy if he thought she would ever blindly obey him. It just wasn't going to happen.

She got the bowls onto the table and got them each a glass of milk. She put the bread and butter out and sat down.

Jack joined her a moment later after washing up, and he looked at the meal. "What's this?" he asked. "It smells good, but I'm curious."

She smiled. "It's a cross between a soup and a stew. Should taste pretty good."

"Interesting. I think I'll like it." He moved the food in his bowl around to see what all was there. "Okay, let's pray."

His prayer was much better that evening. It was more about dealing with conflicts with love instead of asking God to teach her to obey.

After taking a bite of the food, he smiled. "This is really good!"

"I'm glad! I wasn't sure if you'd be okay with me experimenting with different meals, but there are only a few meals with meat I've ever fixed." Grace was determined to get along that evening.

"Well, you're free to experiment any time if your meals turn out like this."

She smiled, happy he was enjoying it. "I think I want to keep the black kitten," she said. "I watch them a lot, and he seems to be calling out to me to love him best."

"Does that mean they can all go back to the barn?"

"Of course not. It's too cold out there. I don't want them to freeze."

He nodded, not surprised that she wasn't backing down about the cats. "I saw you finished the curtains. They look good."

"Thank you. They were very simple, but I think they brighten up the kitchen a great deal."

"Oh, I'm having tea with your sisters tomorrow. Sarah invited me."

"You saw Sarah today?"

"I walked over to talk to her. Elmer gave me a ride back on his standing sleigh. I will never get on that contraption again. I was certain he was going to kill me!"

Jack shook his head. "I'll have to tell him not to drive you on something unsafe."

"I told him I wouldn't ride on it again. He didn't seem to mind." She shook her head. "I had to forge a trail walking over there, and I arrived soaking wet and half frozen. I thought I could walk back along the trail I'd made, but it had already snowed over."

"We get a lot of snow in our valley. You'll see storms like that at least once a week until...well, probably June."

She blinked a couple of times. "Really? Snow in June?"

"Yes. It's happened several times that I remember."

"I'm not sure I'm looking forward to that. I like snow in the winter and warmth in the summer."

Jack smiled. "If I could arrange that for you, it would happen."

"Do you grow crops in the summer?" she asked, trying to steer clear of any subjects that would cause them to fight.

He shook his head. "I make more money by concentrating on my dairy cows. I buy feed from some local farmers. It all works out."

"It sounds like you just focus your time and energy on what you do best."

"I do. There's no reason to do anything else. We have a good community and it's easy to support others by buying what they have to sell. There's no reason for me to grow my own feed."

She smiled and nodded. "That's good! What does this community still need?"

He shrugged. "I think we have everything we need. I mean, I wouldn't mind a store dedicated to tools or to guns, but we can get those things if we're willing to drive a ways."

"And you're willing?"

"Sure. Doesn't hurt me any. I like our peaceful valley, and it wouldn't be the same if there were more businesses. It's perfect just like it is."

Grace nodded. "What little I've seen of it, I like. I'm excited to meet more people at church on Sunday."

"You'll find it's a friendly place to live. We like to have new people, because new people bring more commerce, and we can help each other. I wouldn't live anywhere else."

"I'm sure I'll love it just like you do when I get used to being here. It's so far from home."

"I haven't spoken with Charles yet about a potential bride. I think he'll like the idea."

"Then I'll try to speak to him at church on Sunday." Grace desperately hoped that Sadie could become her real sister and not just a sister of her heart.

"Wait til after church. We always have Sunday dinner at Sarah's, and I don't see that changing just cuz I got married."

"Sounds good to me. Should I take a dish or anything?"

"If you want. A dessert would be most welcome, I think."

Grace smiled and nodded, planning to talk to Sarah about it the following day. What men thought was needed and what women thought was needed were two entirely different things. "I look forward to it."

She'd finished eating so she stood and carried her dish to the basin so she could wash it and get the dishes out of the way. There was plenty of food left for them to have lunch the following day, which would be good. And she could ask Sarah if they sold barley at the mercantile. It would be so nice to have barley. She'd always loved it so much.

After the dishes were done, she checked on the cats before joining Jack in the parlor. To her surprise, Tom followed her with the little black kitten in his mouth.

She sat down and put her hand under the kitten, and Tom dropped it for her to hold. Then Tom was off and bringing another kitten. "Maybe I should move their crate in here..."

"If Tom wants them here, she'll bring them. She knows how."

Grace nodded and snuggled the kitten under her chin. She was determined to keep him forever.

Chapter Seven

Grace was excited about tea the following day. As soon as she'd finished the lunch dishes, she baked some cookies to take as her offering for the tea.

Just before she was about to leave for Sarah's, Jack came into the house. "I hitched up the sleigh. I'll drive you."

"Oh, thank you!" She took one of the cookies from the plate she'd put them on to take them to Sarah's and fed it to him.

He chewed it, smiling. "I may have to get you to make some of these for me."

"I'm glad you like them. These are my favorite."

She walked out to the sleigh and he helped her into it, holding the plate until she was settled, and then giving it back to her. "Thank you for driving me. The snow is much deeper than it was at this time yesterday."

"You're right about that. I'm going to cut more meat from the elk for you to make supper."

"Would you like to cut steaks, and I can make baked potatoes to go with them?"

He nodded. "Can we have bacon on the potatoes again."

"You really do expect me to spoil you, don't you?"

"Well, why else would I send for a wife?" He kissed her, and she laughed.

It only took a couple of minutes to make it to Sarah's but she thanked him for taking the time to drive her.

"I'm going to work with Elmer in his shop while you have tea with the girls, and then I'll drive you back. Just send one of the kids to fetch me."

When Sarah saw the plate of cookies, she smiled. "I almost made cookies, but I decided to make little cakes. Your cookies will be most welcome!"

Another girl who looked to be around Grace's age was with Sarah. "Poppy?" Grace asked.

Poppy nodded. "And you're Grace. It's so good to meet you!"

"And you. I've been looking forward to meeting you all week."

"And I you. But I was busy being a teacher, so I had to wait until Saturday."

No children were in sight, which surprised Grace. "Where are the children?"

Poppy answered for Sarah. "The older boys are with their father helping him. The older girls are upstairs doing something, but no one knows what, and it's honestly probably better that way. And the babies are napping."

"You must enjoy your nieces and nephews," Grace said.

"I enjoy them, but I don't enjoy teaching them. They are always trying to see what kind of trouble they can make at school. Mostly the boys, but the girls get involved sometimes too."

Grace nodded. "It might be better if Sarah stopped having two at a time."

Sarah turned around with the cakes and set them on the table. "I wish I had some say in the matter. One at a time is so much better!"

"Are either of the older sets of twins identical?"

Sarah shook her head. "No, they have different faces and different personalities. I'm thankful I don't have to be confused trying to tell them apart."

"I think that's probably best. There were identical twin girls in the orphanage I grew up in, and they were constantly playing tricks on everyone else. I still wonder what ever happened to them."

Sarah set a small teapot on the table with the cakes and cookies. "I'm so glad you agreed to have tea with us today. We're all sisters now, and it's nice to welcome a new one to the family."

Grace smiled. "I'm happy to have sisters for the first time ever."

As they ate, they told stories about the children and laughed over many things. Grace told of some of the stories from working in the factory, but she made sure to emphasize how her friends and roommates had made working there much easier than it would have been.

"What do the two of you think of me sending for my friend Sadie to marry Charles?"

The two sisters looked at one another, both looking skeptical. "I don't think he's ready for a wife, to be honest," Poppy finally said. "But...there's a man at church that is a widower, has two children, and is looking for a wife. He was envious that Jack found one."

"Then I'll have to meet him and talk to him about Sadie. If Charles isn't ready, then I certainly don't want her to marry him."

Poppy smiled. "Jack was barely ready. I'm sure he gives you fits at times."

"He does!" Grace shook her head. "Soon, I'll have him trained, but it's surprising how long it's taking me. I want him to be trained right now!"

Sarah laughed. "Husband training takes time, but you'll get there. Jack is teachable, I think. I hope!"

For the rest of their teatime, they talked about the community and the type of people she'd be meeting at church the following day. "Just make sure someone introduces me to this Stanley." Grace had a feeling that Sadie would be pleased to help a widower and his two children who no longer had a mother. She'd always loved children.

"I don't think there's going to be a problem there," Poppy said. "He's going to jump at the chance to marry your friend."

"Does he live close?"

"About a mile from here. Not far at all."

"Then I will consider him as a potential husband for my lifelong friend."

Sarah laughed. "Did you think you'd be playing matchmaker when you came here?"

Grace nodded. "I knew I'd be looking for a man for Sadie."

"I hope you find who you're looking for in Stanley." Poppy ate one last cookie. "I'm going to burst if I eat any more, but they're so good!"

Sarah laughed. "They are. I don't know what you put in them, but they are the best cookies I've eaten."

Grace felt a bit of pride overwhelm her. She'd been taught to cook at a young age, but she'd had so little practice over the years. She wasn't sure if she was a good enough cook to marry when she left Massachusetts. Now she knew she was.

When she was in the sleigh going home, she was thinking about Stanley's situation. She hoped that he was still willing to marry someone, because from what Poppy and Sarah had said about him, she felt he would be perfect.

Jack looked at her. "You seem lost in thought."

"I am. Sarah and Poppy suggested that I talk to Stanley tomorrow. They said he would be a good husband for Sadie, and that he really needs a wife."

Jack thought about it for a moment. "I think they're right. Stanley needs a bride to help him. He's a good man."

"I hope he's willing to accept a mail-order bride."

Jack smiled. "He was envious when I told him you were coming. Told me if I had second thoughts to just pass you on."

Grace laughed. "Sounds like he'll be open to it then."

"I think so." He stopped the sleigh in front of the house. "I'll cut those steaks as soon as I unhitch the horse."

"All right." She went into the house and removed her coat, immediately going down into the cellar for the potatoes. She cut off a chunk of the bacon and carried it up as well as the potatoes.

She had just popped her head up through the trap door that led to the cellar when Jack came into the house. "I have the steaks."

Grace had only had a steak once, but she remembered how delicious it was. A local farmer had donated some meat to the orphanage, and the matron had given them all a treat. "Thank you. I look forward to trying an elk steak."

"We don't often have steaks from elk because we're more conservative with our meat than that, but I've had elk steak once, and it was absolutely delicious. Sarah has learned to cook every kind of game there is, and she can do it over an open fire or a fireplace. My sister is a walking marvel."

"I am glad you have a stove. I don't think I could learn to cook over an open fire so easily." She took the steaks from him and set them on a plate. Then she poked holes in the potatoes. Putting the potatoes in the oven, she turned to find Jack watching her. "What?"

He shrugged. "I just...well, I like watching you cook. You're a beautiful woman, Grace."

Grace smiled. "Thank you, Jack. That's very kind of you."

"I'm just telling the truth."

He turned and went back outside to work, but Grace watched him go, pleased that he had said that to her. Until that day, she hadn't known if he was happy with the bride that stepped off the train for him or disappointed. It seemed he was happy.

Jack came into the house around six as usual, his last milking of the day done. "How do you manage to milk so many cows on your own?" Grace asked.

He shrugged. "I've been doing it for a while. Elmer made sure there were always cows around, and he gave me my pick when I decided to start dairy farming. He didn't have a big herd, but I chose ten cows and one bull. That's grown into what you've seen."

"How long ago was that?"

"When I finished school, so I guess I was fourteen. We spent the summer building this house. Anything that looks fancy or special was done by Elmer. Charles and I did the easy stuff."

"Does Charles have a home like yours?" she asked.

He nodded. "It's different but it's just as large and just as nice. He didn't want a second story. He just has the cellar and the main floor."

"Interesting. He's happy there, though?"

Jack nodded. "I believe he is. I also believe he will be a bachelor for a while yet. He's not ready to really settle down and have a family."

She carried their plates from the kitchen into the dining room while he washed, and then she got the butter and the bacon she'd fried and cut into bits. When she sat down, he sat as well, and they prayed and then began their meal.

"You need to give me a list of your favorite foods," Grace said. "I want to know you like what I'm making."

"Maybe we can do that in the parlor after supper. Looks like Tom kept the kittens in there."

Grace nodded. "She did. I give her milk and check on them occasionally, but I haven't tried to move them since I brought them into the house. I think she likes to have them in here."

"It probably is safer for them. No predators and they don't have to deal with the extreme cold. I'm surprised Tom doesn't want to be outside more."

"She asks to go out every few hours, and I let her go. She always comes back within a few minutes though, and goes straight to check on her babies. Tom is a good mama."

"We really need to change her name to something else. Tom is not a good name for a girl."

Grace shrugged. "We could call her Tammy."

He looked as if he was considering the name for a moment, but then he shook his head. "Nah. She's Tom."

"Tom it is." Grace laughed, loving that he didn't know he had a female cat until she gave birth.

Tom must have heard her name, because she walked into the dining room, and then went to the door. "That's my cue to let her out," Grace said. "But you'll see, she really isn't out long." She looked down at her steak. "Is it okay with you if I give her any meat I have left?" She'd given him the large steak, but hers was still much too large for her to be able to finish.

He nodded. "I think that's fine. If my steak had been smaller, I'd want what you have left, but giving it to Tom is the perfect solution."

She cut up the steak she had left and when Tom asked to come back in by scratching at the door, she put the plate on the floor for her. Tom ate it greedily. "Did you need to eat some meat to feed the babies? I'll remember that!"

Jack groaned. "You're spoiling my barn cat!"

"I'm spoiling a new mother with three little mouths to feed." Grace smiled. "I wonder if cats like eggs? I could make extra scrambled eggs in the morning for her."

He shook his head. "Tom will never be the same again. I've heard some farmers say that cats hunt better on an empty stomach, but I've heard others say they hunt better on a full stomach. I guess we'll find out, won't we?"

"We sure will," Grace said, picking up their plates and taking them to the kitchen to wash them. "Oh, no! I forgot to ask your sister if there was something I could take tomorrow to help with Sunday dinner."

"Just make some more of those cookies. If no one else wants them, I'll have no problem devouring them on my own."

She grinned but nodded. "What time is church in the morning?"

"Not til eleven. You could make them in the morning before church if you wanted."

Grace nodded. "That's what I'll do then. I should even be able to get up at my normal time and get them done before we go. Why is church so late?"

"Farmers have morning chores that need to be done before church. I wish I could say that we never work on Sunday, but it's not possible when you're a farmer. Those cows would not be happy if they weren't milked every twelve hours or so."

"That makes sense. I'll bake while you milk cows. Unless you want me to help?"

He shook his head. "No, I'll do the milking. You have enough to do with the cooking, cleaning, sewing, and laundry."

Grace nodded. She had more free time than he realized, but she didn't really have a desire to help milk the cows. If he needed her, she'd be there, but she was glad he didn't need her.

She finished the dishes and went into the parlor with him so she could play with the kittens. Their eyes were still closed, and they had no real ability to play, but it was fun just snuggling them. As long as she remembered that they really were cats and not drowned mice. Sometimes it was hard to remember when she looked at them.

Before bed, she safely tucked the kittens in with their mama. It was a beautiful thing to see Tom nursing her babies and taking care of them the way she did. Grace hoped for the hundredth time that she would be as good a mother as Tom was.

Chapter Eight

At church the following morning, Sarah linked arms with Grace and took her around, introducing her to all the women in the congregation. Then she headed for Stanley. "Stanley's a nice man. Lost his father on the trip here, and his mother married the first captain we had on the trail. She helped him become a much better person."

"Why were there two captains?" Grace asked.

"Actually, there were three. Two of them are here today and the other one moved to where the family had friends. I wonder about his sons, though. They were the most undisciplined children I've ever met." Sarah shook her head. "Actually, I had to tell Jack and Charles not to play with them."

"Oh, my!"

"Here's Stanley." Sarah nodded toward a man who was standing over some children. "Stanley, this is my new sister-in-law, Grace. Grace, this is Stanley Gabriel."

Grace smiled and offered her hand to shake. "It's so good to meet you. I was hoping I could talk to you about something."

"Me?" Stanley looked confused. "Why do you want to talk to me?"

"Well, I was hoping you may want a mail-order bride. You see, my best friend Sadie and I are very sad to be apart. She asked me to find her a man to marry here."

He frowned. "I'll admit I was a tad bit jealous when Jack told me he had a bride coming, but I'm not sure if I'm ready to marry again."

Grace felt her heart sink. "I understand." And she did understand, but she wished things could be different. "Would it help you to know that my friend was raised in an orphanage and she's very used to taking care of children? She's an excellent cook and a good housekeeper. She can even sew well."

"It's not any of that...I would just feel as if I was betraying my wife's memory."

"How long has she been gone?"

"Two years. She died in childbirth and my son died as well."

Grace nodded. "I'm very sorry for your loss. If you change your mind..."

"I really don't think that's going to happen. But I do thank you for the offer. Sometimes I think it would be nice to have a wife, just to mind the children while I'm farming all day. But my mother watches the children, and she tells me they're no trouble, so I'm going to trust her."

"I understand." Grace looked at Sarah sadly. Hopefully there was someone else in town who needed a wife. She'd make a point of being introduced to all the bachelors in town and go from there.

Sarah put an arm around Grace's shoulders as they walked away. "I'm sorry Stanley didn't work out. I think he would be a very good husband to your friend."

"Not if he's still grieving. I don't think that would work at all."

"You're right. Well, I'll introduce you to a few more gentlemen after church. There must be someone."

Grace nodded. "Of course, there is."

She sat with Jack on one end of the family pew, and paid rapt attention to Pastor Scott, who seemed to be called Pastor Jed by most people. "Was he part of your wagon train?" she asked, whispering softly so people wouldn't realize she was talking during church.

Jack gave her an odd glance but nodded once. He obviously didn't approve of her whispering during church, so she sat quietly for the rest of the service, listening to the pastor talk about how the community should work together, reminding them of their arduous journey across the country.

After the sermon, Grace stood and looked around the church. There had to be an unmarried man who wanted to marry Sadie.

She decided not to wait for introductions. She'd heard that people in the west weren't as worried about propriety, and she hoped that was true. Seeing several men leaning up against one wall, she walked over, talking to them each in turn.

Introducing herself as Grace Smith, she explained that she had a friend who wanted to come west to be a mail-order bride.

After talking to six men, the last one said, "I don't know why you're talking to us, ma'am. We're all ranch hands. We live in a bunkhouse. None of us can afford to support a wife right now."

Grace glared at the line of men she'd spoken to who were all watching her. One of them should have told her so she could have gone in search of men who weren't ranch hands. "Thank you for your honesty," Grace said, walking away while shaking her head.

Sarah caught up with her before she made it back to Jack. "What are you thinking talking to all those men alone? Everyone is whispering and talking already."

"I didn't think it mattered. I'm just trying to find a husband for my friend."

"I know, but it didn't look good. I'm sure Jack is quite upset with you by now."

Grace groaned. "But he knows that I'm trying to find a husband for Sadie. Why would he be bothered?"

"Because his wife is talking to men she doesn't know, and she's not waiting for an introduction."

"You're right. I need to be more careful."

Sarah shook her head. "I sure can tell you didn't have a mother governing your actions when you were young."

"No, I didn't. I had something much worse. I wasn't allowed to talk to boys even. We went to school in the orphanage. The only place we even saw boys was at church, and then the matron would take a ruler to our hands if we even looked at one of the boys."

"Oh! I didn't realize that."

"Yes. And once we went to the factory, there was someone else watching over us. I was told manners weren't as strict in the west. I'm a married woman, so I thought it would be all right for me to talk to anyone I pleased." Grace sighed. "I guess I'll wait for introductions."

"I think you're going to have to. I just hope none of the cowboys took what you said wrong. You don't want them coming to visit you while Jack is worki8ng."

"You're right. I really don't want that at all. I hope Jack doesn't think I'm trying to invite them over or something. Now I feel terrible!"

Sarah laughed softly. "Don't. Explain what you were doing to Jack, and all will be fine. I'm sure of it."

Grace wasn't so certain, but she didn't argue with her sister-in-law. Instead, she walked back to Jack and took his hand in hers. "I didn't think I was doing anything wrong. Sarah corrected my misassumption, and I'll never do anything like that again. I'm so sorry." As she apologized, Grace watched his face to see how he was receiving her words.

"We'll talk about it later." Jack's jaw was set, and he looked like he was trying not to start yelling.

Great, Grace thought. *He's angry with me again, and I have no way to convince him that I wasn't intending to do anything wrong. Just when we were getting along well.*

Soon they went out to the sleigh to drive to Sarah's house for Sunday dinner with the whole family. Jack didn't help her into the sleigh, which told her more about his anger than anything else had. "I really am sorry," she said softly.

"I'm not ready to talk about it yet." Jack wouldn't even look at her as he picked up the leads and started driving.

Sunday dinner was very subdued. Everyone could see that Jack was incredibly angry with his new wife, and no one wanted him to redirect his anger. Elmer talked about the weather and a new kind of dresser he was making, and everyone else tried to act as if they were fascinated by what he said, but Grace saw Sarah and Poppy giving her sympathetic glances.

She wanted to shrink down into her chair and hide under the table, but that would be even more conspicuous than her introducing herself to a bunch of cowboys at church. She truly knew better and had no idea why she'd done such a stupid thing.

After the meal she gave Sarah the cookies she'd made, and everyone grabbed one.

Grace smiled as they went so quickly. "It seems that your children are very fond of cookies," she said to Sarah.

Sarah shook her head. "No, Poppy has been bragging about how wonderful your cookies are, and the children are all eager to try them."

Grace said nothing, but she was pleased she'd done at least one thing right since arriving in Clover Creek. She'd been there almost a week, and already she felt like her husband must want to send her back to Massachusetts.

After lunch, everyone sat around and talked for a little while. Everyone but Jack, who maintained a stony silence throughout. When it was finally time to leave, Grace was almost afraid to be alone with her husband. He had waves of anger washing off him.

He didn't speak the entire way home, and he left, slamming the door behind him without a word.

Grace sat quietly for a moment, thinking about how angry she was, but when the tears started to fill her eyes, she got up and started supper. She found some dried navy beans in the basement, and she decided to make them with some bacon. She filled a pot with the beans and bacon and started it cooking and made some rice to go with it.

She knew she would love the meal, and hopefully Jack would enjoy it as well. Not that he could get any angrier with her than he already was.

While the beans boiled, she baked some fresh bread and scrubbed the kitchen floor. She needed to stay busy so she wouldn't worry about the anger that seemed to be consuming her husband.

She knew she must have set a world record. In less than a week she'd made her husband hate her. She only wished she knew how to change his feelings now.

Supper was on the table when he walked into the house. He washed his hands and face and sat down to join her, saying a prayer and then eating in silence.

"I hope you don't mind having beans occasionally. They're inexpensive and very filling," Grace said, hoping it would get him talking to her.

He nodded. "Not a big fan of beans."

"I'll keep that in mind." She glanced at his face, saw it was still stony, and concentrated on her own meal.

After supper, she did the dishes and got everything clean for the next day. "I think I'll go up to bed," she told him. He was in the parlor staring at his almanac but seemed to still be too angry to talk."

He nodded once, and she hurried up the stairs, collapsing on the bed. After a good cry, she changed into her nightgown and laid down to sleep. She had no idea how long it would be before he spoke to her again, but she hoped it wouldn't be too long.

Upon waking the following morning, she realized the other side of the bed hadn't been touched. Apparently, Jack had slept elsewhere.

She decided not to worry and go about her day as usual, so she got up and started breakfast. She decided a hearty breakfast would make him feel better, so she made scrambled eggs, toast, and bacon. Perhaps with all that food in him, he'd be in a better mood. She wasn't sure how he didn't realize that she was incredibly sorry for what she'd done, when she'd told him just that over and over, but he didn't. She would have to see what happened.

He was just coming into the house when breakfast was ready. He set the basket of eggs on the counter and washed his hands and face, going to sit at the table without a word.

Grace served breakfast, leaving a bit of the eggs for Tom. When she sat down beside him, he prayed, and then they ate together. Grace waited until she was almost done with her meal. "Can we just talk about what happened?"

Jack looked at her, and she could see the accusation in his eyes. "Later."

He was acting as if she'd gone to another man's bed when all she'd done was talk to men at church. He was taking things much too far in her opinion.

He finished eating, and stood, putting on his hat and coat, and going out to start his workday. Grace stared at the closed door between them. Surely someday he'd talk to her again.

That day was the longest day of her life. She did the laundry, mended his socks, warmed up the soup from the other night for their lunch, and then she scrubbed the floor of the entire house.

Jack came in, ate lunch, and left immediately, saying nothing to her. The only words he spoke were in prayer.

That afternoon, she baked bread as always, and she made a cake for dessert. Sarah had told her that he was especially fond of sweets, and she was willing to try anything to help his mood.

He dropped another chunk of meat on the counter that afternoon, and she browned it, and then made mashed potatoes, gravy, and corn to go with it. With that and the fresh bread, it should feel like a feast.

That night was the same as the last. She went to bed alone as soon as the dishes were done, and he said nothing to her. She almost wished he'd just start yelling at her and get it over with.

On Tuesday, when she went down the stairs to make breakfast, he hadn't spoken to her in almost two full days. She had no idea what she needed to do, but she knew she needed to do it soon.

At breakfast, she stared down at her food for a moment, and then asked, "Do you want me to go back to Massachusetts?"

His glare made her feel as if he never planned to speak to her again. "Is that what you want to do?"

She shook her head adamantly. "No, I want to stay here with you."

"Then don't ask stupid questions."

Apparently, that was to be the end of their breakfast conversation. It wasn't long before he slammed his hat onto his head and headed out in the cold for the day.

That day she washed all of the windows in the house, stripped all the beds and washed the bedding, realizing he was sleeping in the bedroom across the hall from theirs. She'd remember to make that bed every day, until he was done with his anger toward her. She just hoped that day would come soon.

Chapter Nine

By Friday, Grace was ready to buy a train ticket and head back to Massachusetts. She wasn't sure if she could bear one more day of silence. Every time she asked if they could talk, he told her the same thing. "Later."

On Friday, she walked into town. Thankfully, it wasn't snowing, but it was so cold she hurt. She walked first to the mercantile, and spent a few minutes just looking around the store.

She spotted Stanley Gabriel again, but didn't try to talk to him. She had a feeling she'd spend the rest of her life still married to Jack but back in Massachusetts, working at the mill where she'd spent the last five years of her life.

She found some yarn, and decided to make new socks for Jack before she left. His socks had all been darned too many times for him to keep wearing them comfortably. He hadn't complained, but she knew.

Walking around the store, she chose little things that would make his life more comfortable when she was gone. Then she walked to the train station. "How much would a ticket to Millshore, Massachusetts be?"

The man at the station looked through a book and gave her the price. It was a lot, but she had the money to pay for it. She decided not to buy the ticket until she'd done the things she wanted to do for Jack before she left. Even though they never seemed to see eye to eye, she was in love with the man, and she wanted him to have the best life he could, even though he'd have it without her.

She walked home with her purchases in a crate, getting there just in time to make supper. The elk meat had been distributed to the family, so she didn't know what she would make for supper, but hopefully she could look through the cabinets and something would come to mind.

When she arrived home, there was a slab of meat on the counter. She had no idea what kind of meat it was or where it came from, but she knew it was meant for their supper.

She cubed it and made a thick stew that would hopefully keep them warm through the night.

While the stew was cooking, she sat down with her knitting needles and started on the socks she wanted to make for Jack. She'd make as many pairs as she could with the yarn she'd purchased before leaving. Oh, how it hurt her heart to think of leaving, but wasn't living with a man who refused to speak to her even worse?

When Jack came in after the second milking of the day, she'd finished one of the socks and was about to start on the other. She heard the door and jumped up. "I didn't realize it was so late. I'll have supper on the table in five minutes!"

Sometimes it felt as if she was talking to herself when she said things like that, because Jack never responded, but she was determined to keep things as cheerful as she could under the circumstances.

He spotted the knitting on the kitchen table and glared at her. "What's this?"

"You need new socks, so I was making them for you." She didn't add that she wanted to have several pair for him before she left because she simply didn't want to hear what he had to say about it. The last time she'd mentioned leaving, he told her it was a stupid thing to say.

"Did you put the yarn on my account?" he asked.

"I didn't even think about it," she answered honestly. "I'm used to paying for things myself when I buy them."

"I told you I wanted any purchase you made put on my account. And you walked to the store? It's too cold for you to be wandering around in the snow."

Grace sighed. "I wasn't wandering in the snow. I had a specific destination in mind."

He shook his head and went to wash up for supper, while she got everything on the table.

As they ate, she thought about his promise to take her sledding, and all at once it became the most important thing in the world for her to do. She had to go sledding soon, before she lost her chance. "Could we go sledding tomorrow?"

He turned from soaping up his hands and frowned at her. "Sledding?"

She nodded. "When I first came here, you said you'd take me sledding. I really want to have the experience, if only this once."

He shrugged. "I'll take you then. As long as the weather is fine."

"I know how to bundle up," she said softly. Now that she'd added buying things with her own money to what he already blamed her for, she knew it would soon be time for her to go. Very soon.

She did all her chores while he was milking the cows the following morning, even making the dough she would turn into bread later that day. They had lunch together, and then they set out to go sledding.

He hitched up the sleigh. "We're going to go to the top of that hill," he said pointing, "and then we'll sled down. Charles will have his sleigh as well, and he'll keep taking us back up and meeting us at the bottom until you're finished sledding."

It was the first thing he'd said to her all day, but she had no complaints. She was surprised he was taking his time to do as she'd asked.

At the top of the hill, he set out a sled and then one more. "You take the smaller one."

"Is there a trick to steering this thing, or do I just let go and let God?"

"Don't let go, but there's no steering. You're going to go down the hill, get up, and do it all over again."

"All right." She climbed onto the sled and was nervous for a moment, but then she pushed off and sledded down the hill as if she'd been doing it her entire life. When she reached the bottom, Charles was there to take her back up.

"Did you see me, Charles? I was going so fast!"

Charles laughed. "Sledding is fun, and we have the best hill for it."

"I'm going again!" Grace looked up to see how far she'd come down the hill, and she was amazed. It was like nothing she'd ever done before, and she would treasure the memory of this sledding trip as she sat at her loom weaving.

Jack was there and ready to go again quickly, and Charles drove them up the hill, and they went sledding down. Just before they reached the bottom, Jack's sled crashed into Grace's, and they both tumbled off the sleds and into the snow, Jack landing on top of her.

As soon as she got her breath back, she began to laugh, unable to control the mirth building inside her. To her surprise, Jack began to laugh as well, and he kissed the tip of her nose. She knew he was still angry, but at least they were having a bit of fun together.

He got up, brushed himself off, and held a hand down to help her up. "Are you up for another trip down?"

"Yes, of course!" They picked up their sleds and rushed to Charles's sleigh, climbing on and ready to be taken back to the top.

Charles shook his head. "Are you both all right? That looked like a hard crash."

"I'm fine!" Grace said. "I can't wait to do it all over again."

Jack nodded, his eyes sparkling for the first time in a good long while. "Let's do it!"

Charles drove them up the hill and watched as they unloaded their sleds. "Wait a little longer before you start down, Jack. You don't want to kill your new wife! You just got her!"

Jack stood there, thinking about how he would feel if he lost Grace, and he suddenly felt bereft. There was something so sweet about having supper waiting for him on the table and knowing he had a beautiful woman he could climb in bed with. He tried to think of another woman he'd be happy with, but he couldn't. He was in love with his wife.

He waited until she was out of the way to start down the hill that time. The idea of hurting her, made his heart ache. He'd been a fool to be so angry about something she'd innocently done, but after all this time, he needed to find the right way to tell her that he forgave her.

On his way down, he hit something and went tumbling off again. This time hurt a great deal more. He had no wife to fall on. He cradled his right arm against his body, and saw that his sled was at the bottom of the hill. He would have to make his way down on his own.

He half walked and half fell down the hill, and when he finally reached the bottom, he saw that Charles had stowed his sled in the back of the sleigh. "We're going straight to see Dr. Bentley."

"It's not hurt that badly," Jack protested.

"Don't look at it then. I'm taking you to see the doc."

Jack had no idea what the fuss was about, but he'd go if only to make his brother feel better.

Grace sat beside him, her face white. "I like sledding, but I don't think I like the accidents that go along with sledding."

"I'm fine!" Jack said again, but she could see the blood trickling from the injury above his eye, and the huge bruise on his head. He was hurt a lot worse than he realized.

Charles drove them to Dr. Bentley's home. "I'll take you back to get your sleigh, but you have to be seen by the doc first."

Grace wasn't about to stay in the sleigh when her husband was hurt, so she climbed out of the sleigh and went with him to the door. She knocked loudly, and soon the door opened to a pretty woman who must be in her thirties. "We're looking for the doctor," Grace told her.

"Come in! We met last week at church, but you met so many people I doubt you remember me. I'm Betty, Dr. Bentley's wife and nurse."

Grace was shocked at the sheer number of books that were in the room she was led into. There were shelves all the way to the ceiling, all around the room.

Mrs. Bentley yelled out for her husband. "Malcolm, you have a patient."

The doctor came into the room and took one look at Jack. "What did you do?"

When Jack said nothing, Grace answered for him. "We were sledding, and he fell. His face and his arm seem to be the only injuries."

Dr Bentley led them into a room that was obviously meant for treating patients. "Let's get that coat off you," he said.

Betty went to one side of Jack and the doctor went to the other. They carefully removed his coat, and when Grace saw his arm, she wanted to cry. The bone was very obviously broken, and at a strange angle. "Oh, that looks terrible!"

"It's broken without a doubt," Dr. Bentley said. "You're going to need help with the milking for a while." While he spoke he moved about the room, finding boards and cloth. He carefully cleaned the wound, and then he reached for the arm. "Mrs. Smith, I'm going to need you to wrap your arms around your husband's torso, and hold him as tight as you can."

Grace nodded, feeling terrible that she would be adding to Jack's pain. "Like this?"

"Just like that. Now, do you want a piece of leather to bite down on, Jack?"

Jack shook his head and closed his eyes. He knew a strong pain was coming, and he wanted to be able to take the pain without calling out. He didn't want Grace to think less of him.

"All right. Hold tightly, Grace!"

Grace held to Jack with all her might, feeling Dr. Bentley's pull and fighting it with everything inside her.

"There, it's straight. Let's get that splint on it."

Betty and Dr. Bentley worked in unison to splint the arm, and when they were finished, Jack had sweat standing out on his forehead. "Now I need to look at that cut on your face."

"What cut?" Jack asked, and Grace frowned. How did the man not feel the pain of the cut?

"Your arm is bad enough you probably can't even feel the cut," Dr. Bentley said. He put a clear substance on a rag and used it to dab at the injury. "You're going to have a nice black eye."

The doctor looked at Jack's pupils and did a few other things. "You're going to need to come back to me on Friday," Dr. Bentley said. "I need to make certain your arm is set properly."

"I'll make sure he's here," Grace said. She'd never hitched up a team of horses, but she was going to learn so she could take care of her husband."

"Do you have a ride home?" the doctor asked.

"Yes, his brother Charles is out front." She frowned. "But our sleigh is at the top of the hill."

"Have Elmer help out. It'll be fine."

As they left the doctor's office, Grace felt the guilt roll through her body. Jack had only been out sledding at her request. Now he definitely wouldn't want her to stay.

Charles dropped them off at their home a few minutes later, and promised to be back to take care of the milking that night and in the morning.

Grace said, "I can milk cows."

"You take care of my brother, and I'll deal with the cows," Charles responded. "Get him inside, and I'll get your sleigh home and put the horses up."

Grace nodded, feeling at a loss as to what to do.

She and Jack went into the house together, and she immediately led him into the parlor. "Are you hungry? Can I get you something to eat or drink?"

Jack shook his head, still feeling a bit dazed.

Grace sat down beside him. "I'm so sorry. I never would have asked to go sledding if I'd had any idea this would happen. I seem to only have the ability to mess up your life. I thought I'd make it better."

She would have to put off going back to Massachusetts as she knew he wanted her to do. She would stay and nurse him back to health. It may be the last thing she did for him, but she'd do it with love.

Chapter Ten

For the next four weeks, Grace did everything she could to help Jack. She made him eight pairs of socks and made little pillows for his parlor. When the splint was removed, and he was fully healed, she knew it was time for her to go.

On his first day back to work, Jack smiled at her and asked, "What are your plans for the day?"

"I'm going to buy a train ticket back east," she said, hating to leave him. "I know I'm not the wife you want or deserve, so I'm going to make things easy for you."

"What do you mean?" he asked, obviously shocked.

"I keep doing things you don't like." She couldn't stop thinking about how he hadn't spoken to her for almost a week.

"Oh, Grace, we should have talked about this much sooner. Please don't buy the ticket. I'll milk the cows and come in and we'll talk about everything."

As he left, Grace stood staring at the closed door. Did he want to continue to live under the same roof, but not be truly man and wife? They hadn't made love since before she angered him, and she was certain he no longer wanted to share that with her.

She quickly washed the breakfast dishes and made their beds. He'd kept sleeping in the other room, telling her he was worried it would hurt his arm if she bumped him. She knew it was only an excuse, but she hadn't let on. He didn't want to be close to her, and that was very obvious.

When Grace had finished straightening up the house, she started on laundry. She wanted all his things to be clean before she left, and then he wouldn't have to do it himself or ask Sarah for help.

She was in the cellar hanging his clean clothes when he came in, yelling her name. "Grace! Where did you go!"

"I'm down here!" she yelled back so he could find her.

"Hurry and come back up so we can talk."

"Let me just finish this, and I'll be up."

Grace ascended the stairs a short while later to find him in the parlor, not reading the almanac as usual, but just staring off into space. "I finished the laundry. It's drying in the basement. I'll get it ironed before I go."

Jack looked sad at her words. "Sit with me," he said.

Grace took the seat beside him on the sofa but made sure to keep space between them. He hadn't wanted to touch her, and she wasn't about to beg for his affection.

He looked over at her, a sad look on his face. "I'm not angry with you," he said softly. "You have taken care of me while my arm was broken. You've made me socks and made my home feel so much better. All the little things you do for me please me. You're what I wanted in a wife and so much more."

"But...You haven't slept in our bed for weeks!"

"My arm was broken, and I worried that you would roll onto it in the night. I planned to return to our bed tonight, now that the doctor has removed the splint, and I know it's all right."

She bit her lip. "But I talked to all those cowboys."

"You did. And I was very angry at the time. But you didn't take care of the cowboys. You haven't even glanced their way since that first week at church. And though you don't always obey me, you make me feel like you love me with everything you do."

Grace tilted her head to one side, looking at him. "I do love you."

He smiled. "And I love you!"

She looked at him skeptically. "Are you only saying that because you don't want me to go? Because if you are, I think it's cruel. You don't have to say it simply because I did."

"No, I don't have to." Jack shook his head. "I realized that day sledding that I loved you. After I crashed into you, I watched you go down the hill the next time, and I thought about how much better my life is with you in it. I tried to imagine any other woman I'd want to spend my life with, but I knew then that there would never be anyone I loved but you."

"But you never said anything!"

"I didn't, and that's where I went wrong. I promised myself I'd talk to you, but then I hurt myself and we had to see the doctor, and…I just never got back around to it. If I'd known you were thinking of leaving, I'd have told you long ago."

Grace sighed. "I could have said something too, but I thought you hated me. Especially since you hurt yourself taking me sledding. I wanted to go. You didn't!"

"You're wrong about that," Jack said. "I wanted to be there the first time you went. To see the excitement on your face and to laugh with you. When I crashed into you, and we both started to laugh, I felt for the first time in my life that everything was right with the world."

Grace stood and moved closer to him. "Thank you for not giving up on me."

"I couldn't. I love you too much."

Grace rested her head on his shoulder, feeling as if she never wanted to move away from him. "But you know what this means? I have to find a husband for Sadie!"

He chuckled. "Let me ask around. You don't need to meet strange men and try to get them to marry your friend. Tell me everything you can think of about her, and I'll ask around at church."

"Oh, thank you! That would make me so happy!"

"And you won't be putting yourself in awkward positions. I want to meet this Sadie of yours. It sounds to me like she's an amazing person to have inspired so much loyalty in you."

She sighed contentedly. "I guess I should go get lunch ready."

"You can do that. Or you can go upstairs with me, and I'll show you how very much I love you and want you here!"

"That sounds better to me. Let's go!"

THREE MONTHS LATER, Grace was waiting for him as he walked in the door after the evening milking. She raised her lips for his kiss.

He leaned down and kissed her. "You're not in the kitchen. You're always in the kitchen."

She smiled. "I wanted to talk to you before we eat."

"Why is that?" Jack stole one more kiss and waited for a response.

Grace took his hand and pulled him into the parlor with her, sitting with him on the sofa. "I haven't been feeling well, as you know, so I finally went to the doctor today."

Jack's eyes widened. "Are you all right? Is there something wrong with you?"

She laughed and shook her head. "Not a thing is wrong with me that nine months won't fix."

He drew his brows together. "Nine months?" And then her meaning dawned on him and he stared at her for a moment before letting out a loud, "Whoop!"

She laughed at his reaction. "I hope I don't take after your sister and have a bunch of sets of twins."

He smiled, kissing her. "We'll all hope for that. Twins are a lot of work!"

"They are." She stood up. "Let me get supper on the table."

As he watched her walk away, he thought about how different life would be if she wasn't in it. All the love he felt for her clamored inside him, and he knew he could never let her go. She was his.

Epilogue

My dear friend Cecelia,

I hope this letter finds you well. I have news for you to impart for me. I'm expecting a baby in the fall. Please tell all the other girls and Mrs. Durant. I miss all of you every day, but I'm very happy here in Clover Creek with my Jack.

I hope you'll do as Josephine, Rebecca, and I have done and put an ad to find a husband. Married life is truly blissful now that Jack and I have worked out our differences. If you do move west to marry, please be careful to work through your differences and not plan to run back to Millshore. As much as I hated it there, I was once ready to go back to working at the mill.

Open communication is the most important thing. And if your husband is stubborn as mine, you may have to sit on him to get him to talk to you.

I can't wait to hear how things are going there, and I eagerly await your next letter.

Sincerely,
  Grace